Heart of the Mountain

Heart of the Mountain

A short novella

Jeanette O'Hagan

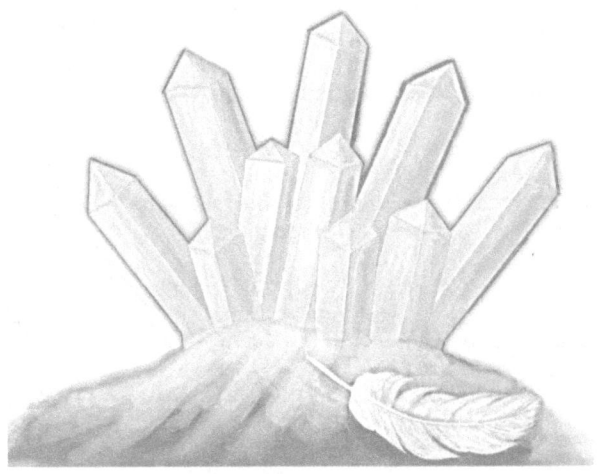

Story 1 Under the Mountain series

By the Light Books

Heart of the Mountain: a short novella
By Jeanette O'Hagan
Sotry 1 in the Under the Mountain series

Cover design: Jeanette O'Hagan © 2016
Typesetting and Layout: Jeanette O'Hagan
Copyright Jeanette O'Hagan © 2016/2017
http://jeanetteohagan.com

National Library of Australia Cataloguing-in-Publication entry

Creator: O'Hagan, Jeanette, author.

Title: Heart of the mountain : a short novella / by Jeanette O'Hagan.

ISBN: 978-0-9943989-9-4

Series: O'Hagan, Jeanette. Under the mountain ; Story 1.

*Subjects: Fantasy fiction.
Orphans--Fiction.
Shapeshifting--Fiction.*

Dewey Number: A823.4
ISBN-13: 978-0-9943989-9-4

Published through By the Light Books
By the Light Books PO Box 2520, Brookside Centre, Qld 4053
Email: Bythelightbooks@gmail.com

Note: This book follows Australian style conventions for spelling, punctuation and grammar.

Subscribe to Jeanette O'Hagan's Newsletter for the latest on new releases, giveaways and other news– http://eepurl.com/bbLJKT

This story is in memory of my brother Chris much loved, missed and never forgotten.

An updraught caught Zadeki and flung him about like a spinning leaf. Clouds of snow blasted into his face, ruffling his feathers and blinding him. Another gust hit him side on, pushing him off balance. It had been a foolish decision to fly over the mountains. The clear blue sky of the early afternoon was a fading memory as he was caught up in a world of swirling snow and ice. If only he could find shelter, but even with his eagle-sharp eyes, he could see no more than a white fuzzy blur in every direction. Gathering his trembling muscles and spreading out his flight feathers, he fought against the might of the wind.

As the whiteout lessened for a few moments, a sharp angular peak loomed in front of him. His heart racing, he tilted his wings in a desperate attempt to turn. His flight pinions clipped a ledge. He lurched. His right side slammed into the icy rock, sending him spiralling down, ricocheting off the sheer cliff face. Pain screamed through him as fragile wing bones snapped. All control of his descent vanished. So much for showing the Kinleader he was old enough to be a pathfinder. His thoughts frayed and darkness took him.

Delvina clutched her brother's thick felt jerkin. The air was strange in these outer tunnels, laden with the smell of strange resin and a bitter icy bite she was not used to. A gust ruffled her bangs, sending a shiver through her.

'Are you sure we should do this, Retza? The outside is dangerous.'

'Shush. It will be more dangerous if we're caught.'

She lowered her voice. 'Who would hear us? No one's stupid enough to come out this far.'

As Retza rounded a corner, he pulled to such a sudden stop that she bumped into him.

'What is it?' she hissed.

A pale yellow glow came from the end of the tunnel—different from the dancing smoky red of flame or the focused cool blue of the glimmer lights. It illuminated Retza's snub nose and glistened in his wide eyes, his pupils contracting to slits against the sudden glare.

'Sunlight?' Her voice caught in her throat.

Retza grunted. 'Maybe. Come on, we can't give up now.'

They shuffled along the tunnel as the circle of light ahead of them brightened. Delvina shaded her eyes, her mouth dry. Why had they thought this was a good idea?

A freezing wind blasted Retza's face as he poked it out of the entrance. He gripped the tunnel walls and squinted at the white blur outside. Delvina pressed up behind him, her grasp on his jerkin almost choking him, her breath warm on his ear. He took a deep breath. He was glad his twin sister was with him though he wasn't going to admit it to her.

A flurry of white flakes swirled in front of his nose. Putting out a hand he caught one. It melted away to a tiny tear drop in his calloused palm. As his eyes adjusted, he could make out mounds of the soft white substance smothering the world outside. The open space of the Cauldron went up, and up, higher than even the Grand Cavern. Above the sharp rim, grey streamers raced against a black sky studded with pinpricks of light like ribbons of glow worms on a cave roof. A shudder ran through him. The outside was even stranger than he had imagined.

A swathe of the grey stuff thinned, revealing a round burnished disk of bright golden light.

He pointed. 'The sun.'

Delvina cleared her throat. 'It's not bright enough to be the sun. And look there's another one.' She pointed to another disk, further down in the chaotic expanse above their heads. It winked back at them; silverly, almost as bright, and misshapen, like a mushroom with an edge shaved off. 'I think they are both moons.'

'Yes, two moons ... that's what I meant to say. So where's the sun?' He scanned the sky.

'Maybe it's night.' His twin's voice quivered on the last word.

He swallowed against the lump in his throat. If this was night, then what would the day be like? 'We'd better stop wasting time.' His voice was harsher than he had intended.

They pushed out into the open, wading through soft mounds that slumped to the side and muffled the sound of their footsteps. Sweeping aside the piles with his hands, he rummaged around, picking up and discarding rocks, spindly sticks and other debris. Soon his clothes were soaked, his fingers aching and numb. His sister's pale face had a bluish tinge around her lips and her chin was shuddering.

A sullen dread settled inside him. It was supposed to be such a simple challenge—sneak outside and find something unusual to give to the Greenstone South Crew. If it was good enough, perhaps he and Delvina would be accepted as prentices. But it could take hours to find anything under this thick blanket of fluffy wetness.

He thrust his frozen hands under his armpits and ground his teeth. 'This is useless.'

Delvina didn't respond. She was poking a stick behind a spur of rock jutting out from the sheer cliffs that enclosed the Cauldron. Her long ash blonde plait fell like a thick rope down her back, a pale streak against the matted brown of her jerkin. If they didn't find something their quest would have failed, but if they stayed out here much longer they would freeze to death.

His sister squealed and jumped back.

'What is it?' He pressed through the path her body had cleared.

'It moved.'

She pointed at a heap of white and dark grey fronds that blended into the white stuff and the grey of the rock behind. He leaned forward. The delicate fronds were like feathers of the small cave birds, only larger. Some of them were stuck together with a dark red substance. She poked it with the stick again.

The mound shifted, a large wing-like object fluttering. He breathed in sharply. Feathers, wings and, now that he thought about it, he could see the hooked beak with sharp tip and closed eyes. Its other wing was bent at a strange angle.

'It's a bird.' His twin sister clucked her tongue. 'And it's hurt.'

'It's so big.' The swifts and swallows that nested in the

upper caverns and sometimes became trapped in those beneath were a mere mouthful. This bird was almost as big as they were. Excitement bubbled up in his chest.

'We can take it back.'

Delvina's speckled face split into a grin. 'Yes, it's injured. We can help it.'

He thumped her shoulder. 'Silly. It's our trophy—for the challenge.'

She shook her head. 'It wouldn't survive long in the caverns. We should tend it and release it when its wing is healed.'

He rubbed his icy hands together, excitement mounting. 'Yeah, but it's dying anyway and look how big it is. Plenty of meat and feathers. Have you any idea how many crystals that's worth. The Crew will have to induct us.'

Her brow furrowed. 'I guess.'

'Here, help me catch it.' He shouldered out of his jerkin. They each took a corner, spread it out like a net and walked towards their prey.

An eye, black as coal, snapped open and stared back at him.

He paused. 'Perhaps we should brain it first.'

Crouching, he picked up a large rock lying in the cleared area in front of the spur.

In a flurry of movement, the bird catapulted backwards, banging into the cliff behind. Its wings pumped downwards or at least one did, while the other thrashed uselessly. It gave a long keening whistle.

It stretched upwards, its outline blurring and dissolving until a tall, skinny figure stood half cantered against the rock wall.

'Don't kill me.'

Zadeki's heart was just about jumping out of his chest, his limbs still tingling. He gritted his teeth against the screaming throb where bone ends had torn flesh in the sudden, almost instinctive transformation. His right arm dangled at his side.

The white swathed landscape and the two pale faces seemed to pitch and roll as though floating on the ocean. He sucked in a huge lungful of frigid air, triggering a deep shuddering through his body. He was cold to the core and a deep weariness settled over him, yet fire seared along his right side. Not good to change shape under such conditions but what else could he do? He was sure he'd heard the words 'eat it' and 'brain it'.

Slowly, the world came into focus. Two round faces, with gaping mouths and a soft scattering of speckles across their snub noses, stared at him. Their great round eyes looked as colourless as water in the subdued moonshine. They barely came up to his armpit. The gruffer one had a fuzz on his chin and upper lip while the other had suggestive shapes beneath the baggy clothing of her shabby jerkin, tunic and breeches. Both were sturdily built. Young ones like himself, on the cusp of adulthood.

The one with the fuzz recovered from his shock first. He ran a pink tongue over his blue-tinged lips, and then his face split into a toothy leer. 'Can we help you, above-grounder?

Zadeki snorted. 'Into the pot. I can do without that sort of help, earthbiter.'

'Did you just change from a bird to a ... well, whatever you are?' The other one, with the long plait of pale hair asked. The girl's eyes were even wider than her companion's, her voice soft with wonder.

Despite the occasional flurry of snow, the blizzard was gone. Trouble was he couldn't afford to change shape while injured even if he had the energy to do it—and even if he could fly with one arm broken. But surely he could climb out of here, as long as he didn't freeze first. He scanned the high cliff face that curved around like pincers. The exit out of the valley must be on the other side, though he could see no break in the rim.

'Yes. Can you show me how to get out of here?'

'There is no way out of the Cauldron,' the girl said. 'Besides, you need help.' She pointed at his damaged arm.

He narrowed his eyes. 'You might eat me.'

Her face split into a smile. 'We don't eat people.'

The boy snarled. 'Just leave him, Delvina. We're wasting time.'

'We can't leave him to die here.'

He shrugged 'He's not of the People. Who knows, maybe this white stuff is what he lives on.'

Zakeki snorted. 'Who lives on snow?' The girl was right, he couldn't survive out here, not without shapeshifting. Yet would he be any safer in the caverns? He doubted it.

The young male looked mutinous. 'How would we get him past the watchers?'

Delvina thrust out her chin. 'The same way we did. Come on Retza. Otherwise we have nothing to prove to the Crew that we came here, and the outsider needs our help.'

'This is not the same as tending an injured bat or keeping a cave cricket.' But the one called Retza cast aside the rock he held in his hand. 'You better keep up, stranger. If the watchers come after us, you're on your own.'

A smile trembled on the girl's lips. 'Don't mind my brother. He has a heart of gold, really.' Taking Zadeki's hand, she pulled him towards the dark opening of a cave some hundred paces away. He followed, clenching his teeth against the pain shooting through him with each step and every breath. What other choice did he have?

Zadeki had to stoop as he followed the two Darane (for surely they were the ancient mountain dwellers) trundling ahead of him. A line of blue, glittering lights ran along the walls. The floor was mostly smooth and had a consistent downwards incline taking him deeper into the heart of the mountain. The biting wind did not reach far into the passageway and soon the shudders that racked his body lessened into an occasional shiver.

After a while, the tunnel opened into another higher one. Delvina grabbed his left arm and whispered in his ear. 'Don't step on the plate. It triggers an alarm.' She pointed to a square of dull metal set in the floor where the tunnels joined. 'And if you see a watcher, run.'

'Why? What will they do to us?'

Retza's hiss echoed off the walls. 'Us? There is no us. The outer passages are out of bounds, and transgressors are killed on sight.'

'Then what were you doing outside?'

'Stop your yakking and jump.' The fellow then leaped over the plate, disappearing around the corner. Delvina followed.

Zadeki swallowed hard. Normally, the jump would be simple but in his present condition even walking was hard. Maker help him, what was he getting himself into? A calmness flooded him. *Follow*. Holding his injured arm against his chest, he leapt over the plate, teetering on the other side until Delvina grabbed him.

She pulled him along the path with a surprising strength. The roof of this tunnel was higher than the last, allowing him to walk without stooping. The Darane led him through a maze of passages and down long spiralling stairs. At last the tunnels opened up into more cavernous hallways. At first one or two, then large groups of the sturdy under-mountain people streamed around them. Most of the men had braided beards while the woman wore their pale hair in long plaits. Dressed in drab, serviceable clothes and carrying tools or bearing large baskets, the people kept their lamp-like eyes to the ground.

The Darane lass looked over her shoulder and hissed. 'Hunch over. Don't draw attention to yourself.'

How could he not? He had never been more out of place in his life. But he hunched as best he could, gasping at the knife-like stabs in his chest. Eventually, they entered a huge cavern with a roof high as the giant forest trees. Large stone spikes clung to the rock ceiling and down the middle of the chamber came the chuckling flow of a river that ran in a deep channel below. Built into the walls were open counters piled with tools, clothing or food and between them, doors to more secluded rooms.

Zadeki stumbled as the lights flickered. Both Retza and Delvina stopped walking, tipping back their heads to look at the big lamps attached to the wall and pillars. Even as he blinked, the cavern was plunged into blackness.

'Not again,' Retza muttered.

Zadeki's heart fluttered against his chest. He swallowed a scream. It was hard enough coping with the enclosed space and weight of rock above his head without darkness so deep he couldn't see his hand in front of his face. His breathing quickened. Slowly, he could make out small points of light above him. They couldn't be stars, surely? 'What are they?'

'Glow worms,' the girl said, her voice pitched higher than normal. 'The glimmer lights normally hide them.'

With a whump, the lights flooded back on again. A murmur of relief ran through the Darane, like a wind through tree branches of the forest canopy. They continued their hurried movements, some bumping and shoving as they flowed around Zadeki and the two Darane youngsters. If only he were with his kin now, instead of deep in the bowels of the mountains. He might die down here and they would never know what happened. Never had he been so alone.

Delvina tugged at him. 'Come on, above-grounder, the Greenstone South's crib is further down the Great Causeway.'

Some lengths later, they turned into a corridor and hammered on a rusted metal door.

Retza's hand shook as he pounded on the door. He jumped back a pace as it shot open with a clang. Secondwun Putarn stuck his head out and squinted at them.

'Whatcha want, youngwuns?'

Retza licked his lips. 'Secondwun, we...' Fear clenched his belly. They would only get one chance at this. The gangly stranger was unusual, but would he be enough to impress Lead Hand Havilah?

The Secondwun snorted and began to close the door.

Delvina jumped past him and stuck her boot into the doorway.

'We bring a trophy. We have a right to present it to your Lead Hand.'

The man stroked his plaited beard, then stepped back. 'Come in.'

Retza met his sister's gaze. This was it. He grabbed the above-grounder and pulled him inside. A number of crew members, toolwuns mostly, were sitting at the fixed tables and chairs on one end of the crib room. Some played table games—cards, knuckle bones or counters. Some were chatting or mending worn garments. They looked up for a moment before returning to their activities. Behind them, a grey felt curtain was pulled across the dormitory area where other members of the crew would be sleeping. The crib hadn't changed much since he'd last seen it, just before their parents were killed. Retza swallowed against the tightness in his throat.

Putarn disappeared into the entrance to the ward room on the other side of the long rectangular room.

Retza turned to Delvina and attempted a smile. She nodded once, her face tight with fear. The above-grounder was clutching his arm to his side and shivering. Dried blood clotted in his pitch-black hair and his right temple. His dark eyes flitted about the room. Then, with a soft sigh, he slid down the wall and rested his head in the crook of his left elbow. It was clear that the fellow was in a bad way. Without asking, Delvina stomped across the room where hot gruel bubbled in the big pot on the hob. She ladled it into a tin mug, before stumping back and giving it to the above-grounder.

Retza scuffed the wall with his worn-out boots. It was just like Delvina to get attached. She had a soft heart for anything in trouble, but they could not afford such sentimentality. Ever since their parents' deaths a few years back they'd been on their own. They needed to pass this challenge. The lives of the crewless were short and brutal.

His sister crossed to the pot again and returned with two steaming mugs. The faint aroma of mushrooms wafted towards him and his stomach rumbled. Grunting his thanks, he blew across the surface of the brew and sipped.

It was a while before Putarn emerged, followed by his mother, Lead Hand Havilah, and the old Scrybe. The Hand ran strong fingers through her grey-streaked hair before pulling up an ancient wooden chair. Her pale amethyst gaze flicked towards them, but showed no recognition. Retza let out a long breath. He and Delvina had been just littlewuns that last time they'd come to the crib but he had hoped she'd remember them. He looked down at the stone floor, polished smooth from generations of feet. Would all their efforts be for nothing?

Scrybe Barekia shuffled over to a recessed shelf carved into the wall, lifted out the huge records book and placed it on a stand. She opened it out and smoothed down the precious pages with two wrinkled hands.

The Hand leaned forward. 'Who have we here, Secondwun?'

Putarn cleared his throat. 'Let the candidates step forward and state their names.'

'Retza, son of Toolwuns Zalell and Holima, formerly of your crew, Lead Hand. And this is my twin sister, Delvina.'

The Lead Hand's eyelids flickered. 'Yes, yes, Zalell and Holima.'

'Why aren't the toolwuns here to sponsor their offspring?' Putarn growled.

'They were killed in ... the cave-in.' The Scrybe ran her blunt finger down a list of names. She looked up, her eyes gentle. 'These are indeed their offspring. They have the right to try as prentices with our Crew.'

Havilah sucked in a breath and spread her hands out on her knees. 'Present your trophy, applicants.'

Thirdwun Nebam called from the tables. 'What weevilly booty have you found, runts?' The other toolwuns erupted into catcalls and whistles.

The Secondwun sniggered at his brother's joke before remembering his duties. 'Quiet, you lot.' He turned to the twins. 'Come on, the Lead Hand hasn't all day.'

Retza licked his lips. 'We went outside to the Cauldron. And there was white stuff ...' He took a deep breath.

'I think it was snow,' Delvina said. 'Snow all over.'

Retza nodded. 'And an injured bird.' All eyes were on them now. 'But he changed into ...'

'... to him.'

Both twins pointed to the above-grounder sitting on the floor, watching them.

A collective sigh swept through the room.

'A bird would be more useful.' The Hand sat back in the chair.

Gripping his belt with both hands, Retza held his breath. Please by whatever powers that be, let the trophy be accepted. A feeling of unease niggled at his thoughts. Their trophy looked too fragile to work hard as a drudge and only the Overseer kept mascots. What else could they do with him?

Putarn poked the above-grounder. 'Not much meat on his bones.'

The stranger stood shakily to his feet, his left hand gripping the wall. 'My name is Zadeki. I'm sure I can help you somehow in exchange for showing me the way out of here.'

Lead Hand Havilah gave a low guttural laugh. 'The Old Overseer closed the gates nigh on two hundred years ago. Since then no one has come in or out.'

As she spoke, the glimmer lights in the low ceiling flickered. A murmur ran through the room. The Lead Hand's eyes remained fixed on the above-grounder. Then as if in response to the flickering, a heavy hammering resounded on the metal door. Havilah broke her gaze and flicked her fingers towards the door. Putarn rushed to open it. A messenger pushed inside.

'Lead Hand of the Greenstone South Crew?'

Standing up, Havilah smoothed down her robes. 'Yes?'

He thrust a message cylinder at her. She unlocked it with the key around her neck, and scanned the copper foil pages. Handing it to the Scrybe, she stood up.

'Secondwun, come with me.'

Retza grabbed her sleeve. 'What about us?'

The Thirdwun grunted. 'Shall I have these hopefuls thrown out?'

Havilah turned, squinting through narrowed eyes. 'No. Any youngwuns brave or maybe stupid enough to dare the Cauldron deserve a chance to prove themselves. We could do with some after losing the last ones. Scrybe Barekia, assign these youngwuns a bunk and kit each, and see they are fed. Make sure the above-grounder is cared for.'

Retza whooped. He grabbed Delvina's arms and spun her around. They'd done it. They'd found a berth in the Crew.

The Lead Hand snorted. 'You're on probation as trywuns, mind you. And wait until you get your duty roster. You might not be hooting so loudly then.'

She and Secondwun Putarn strode out into the dim corridor, the door clanging shut behind them.

Probation? Trywuns, not real prentices yet? Retza let out a long breath. At least they had half a foot in the door.

Hot and cold chills raced through Zadeki. The heat of the thin gruel the girl had given him earlier had at least calmed the shivers racking his body. It was warm in this room too, almost stuffy. Delvina and Retza, visible through gaps of the felt curtain, stood beside their assigned bunks. Their ash blond heads touched as they sorted through their kits. The other Darane had turned back to their drinks and pushed bits of card and round counters about on the stone tables; no longer, it seemed interested in him. Close by, the old woman pored over the time-stained book, her thin lips pursed. For the moment, no one seemed to be paying him any attention. What did the earthbiters mean to do with him? Surely, they wouldn't eat him? He pulled his mantle more tightly around his shoulders and rested his head against the cool stone wall. Swirls of snow flashed beneath his closed eyelids as he drifted on a sea of pain.

He jumped and winced as a gravelly voice sounded in his ear.

'You're one of Doryn's Kin, aren't you?' The wrinkled face and gapped tooth smile of the one they called Barekia leered at him. 'An Adelphi?'

'Yes, earth mother.' He looked at her warily, flinching back as she leaned forward to finger his hair and stroke his skin. She gently touched the abrasions on his forehead.

'What happened to you?'

'I flew into a mountain side.'

She chuckled. 'Not a good idea.'

He lifted his chin. 'There was a blizzard.'

'No doubt.' She turned and called. 'Trywun Delvina, bring some warm water. Retza, get me some rods, clean cloth and stagmoss from the top shelf of the recess.'

Delvina jumped up and ladled steaming water from the pot on the hob into a stone basin. Retza, a scowl on his pallid face, was slower to move.

The old woman turned back to Zadeki, her voice pitched for his ears only. 'I was present, though only a youngwun, when the current Overseer's father ordered the front gates to be sealed up.'

Zadeki shuffled, trying to find a more comfortable position for his throbbing arm. 'My baba and matu speak of it. My kin could not fathom the reasons why your people broke contact. We feared you had perished.'

'The Dark Ones commanded it. You best beware, young shapeshifter. You are out of your depth here.'

'Don't I know it?' He grimaced. What did she mean Dark Ones? Were they the Shadow Eaters of Light or some other malevolent beings? But that wasn't his worry. He just needed to get out of here. 'Could you show me where the gate is?'

'I could, but it wouldn't help you much. It is well guarded and even better sealed. There is no way to get past it.'

He swallowed, a sinking feeling in his gut. He had to get out with or without the help of the Darane. 'Surely there are other exits?'

'There is no other way out of the Glittering Realms. Shush.'

The two youngsters arrived with the steaming water, bandages and other items. Retza stomped back to his bunk, but Delvina hovered behind the old woman.

Barekia pulled a globule of gum from a dented tin box and handed it to Zadeki. 'Chew this. It will numb the pain.'

Zadeki shook his head. He needed his wits about him. 'No thanks.'

She sniffed. 'Have it your way, Adelphi. Delvina, hold him still.'

Before he could protest or move, the stumpy old woman had grabbed his right arm and pulled it. He yelped as pain seared through him. His vision darkened at the edges and then sweet relief filled him as the bone ends fitted back into place and the agony subsided to a dull ache. The old woman splinted his arm with the rods, winding stripes of tough felt around his arm to hold the splint in place. Next she tended his forehead, dabbing it and coating it with a dark paste.

'Anywhere else?'

'Just a couple of cracked ribs but ...'

He flushed as she lifted his tunic, exposing the deep purple-blue bruising along his right side—from collar bone to thigh.

'Humph, I'll mix up a poultice. That should help.' Her fingers lingered on the fabric of his tunic, a gleam lighting up her pale eyes. 'Fine cotton. Only Overseer Uzza, his family and favoured servants sport such rare fabrics these days.'

He blinked. Of course, cut off from the outside world, there would be many things the Darane no longer had access to. Most of all sunlight and fresh air. It was a wonder they survived at all in these dim, claustrophobic tunnels.

He pulled down his tunic. 'Thank you for your care, earth mother.'

She chuckled and poked a bony finger between his ribs. Looking over her shoulder, she spoke to Delvina. 'You girl, get this skinny post something solid to eat. There's naught but skin on his lanky bones.'

The others sitting at the table cackled until Zadeki's cheeks burned. His stomach lurched. Despite their squat frames, none were fat and a look of hunger lurked in their pale eyes.

Delvina stifled a yawn. She ached all over from last period's shift, shovelling the ore into glimmer trucks. The last several days had been crammed working the Greenstone South roster followed by exhausted sleep. In the down times, she and Retza were expected to serve the other toolwuns and do the basic cleaning. It was hard work but better than the back-breaking dangerous tasks assigned to the drudges. And at least here she had a chance of a safe place to sleep and regular food. Besides, if they complained, the Lead Hand might let them go. Her stomach knotted as she stirred the bubbling pot. They were only on probation. Replacing the lid, she bent down and pulled out three ration parcels from the food locker.

'Retza.' Her brother lifted up his head from where he was scrubbing the floor. 'Break time.' She threw him one. Then sidled over to where Zadeki sat cross legged on the floor. His arm was in a sling and while his skin was still a silvery white, he looked less peaked. He had recovered remarkably well, the deep purple mottling on his face already fading to a pale yellow.

He looked up at her, his dark eyes bright, until he saw the wrapped parcels. He groaned.

'Not more algae cakes?'

He took it, anyway. Wrinkling his straight nose, he nibbled a corner with his strong, white teeth.

She settled herself beside him. 'If you don't want it, I'd be happy to eat your share.'

His eyes widened and he shook his head vigorously. 'I'm hungry enough to eat rocks, if that was all you had to offer.'

She laughed. 'Nothing seems to fill you up.'

He nodded solemnly and licked his lips. 'What I'd do for some plump berries—or fish seared in the fire, eaten under the stars and the moons.'

'Fish? Only the Overseer's household gets fish. Are you from a leadwun's family then?'

He tilted his head to one side. 'My great-grandmother is Kinleader but my people eat fish all the time.' He leaned back against the wall, a wistful look clouding his face.

'You miss your family.' She bit her lip. She missed her own parents. Not for the first time she wondered what the Lead Hand planned for the above-grounder. She hoped it wasn't too harsh a fate. As if sensing her mood, the glimmer lights flickered for a few moments. It had been happening a lot lately.

Zadeki leaned forward. 'Things aren't going too well for your people, are they?'

She stiffened. 'Why do you say that?'

'Food is hardly plentiful and materials are scarce. And then the lights keep failing. What would you do if they go out?'

Her stomach dropped like lead. What a horrible thought.

'They won't go out.' Retza stood in front of them, a scowl on his face. 'That's trash talk. Besides, the lights have been flickering since before we were littlewuns.'

Delvina nodded. 'Yes, it's nothing unusual.'

Well, perhaps they were becoming more frequent. She shifted, trying to find a more comfortable position on the hard floor. A niggling voice teased her. Maybe securing a permanent berth in the Crew wasn't the only thing to worry about. No, the Overseer and the leadwuns had things under control.

Zadeki shrugged. 'But what about all these hushed meetings, the smell of desperation, the hurried looks?'

Retza jutted out his jaw. 'You're imagining things, above-grounder. You should be more worried about what's going to happen to you. The other toolwuns are already muttering about wasting resources on a freeloader.'

And then the lights went out. And stayed out. The crib room was as black as the deepest pit, not a glimmer of light except for the hint of luminescence of the above-grounder's skin. Retza's heavy breathing tickled Delvina's ear and his hand found hers. Across the room, the toolwuns shuffled and coughed in their seats. Small sounds seemed overloud; the simmering of the pot on the hob, the muted cry of a littlewun from the Causeway. The moments dripped by and a weight on her chest pressed down, growing heavier and heavier. What if the lights never came back on? But they always had before. Besides, they could light torches or lamps. She chewed her knuckle, willing the lights to return.

A flicker showed strained faces, eyes wide with fear.

A plunge back into darkness and then the steady, unwinking blue shine of the glimmer lights filled the silent room. After a brief outburst of fevered comments, the others turned back to their games, mending and conversations.

Delvina met Zadeki's deep eyes. Perhaps he was right. But what could anyone do?

Retza gulped down the last of his ration cake before going back to his chores. He sloshed the water on the floor, attracting a few curses from the nearby toolwuns, and scrubbed the polished stone surface vigorously. It was true that the flickering and rare blackout had been going on for years, yet this was the second blackout in twelve days and the flickering was increasing in frequency. And Havilah had the Crew on reduced rations. He sat back on his heels and stretched his back. When he'd asked Putarn about it, the Secondwun had clipped him over the ears and growled that he and Delvina were welcome to return to the commons, if they wished. That wasn't an option! Retza's muscles tightened like ropes and the sparse meal sat uneasily in his stomach. Blast it, he shouldn't let the above-grounder unsettle him. What did he know after all?

He glanced over to where his sister sat next to the tall fellow, their heads together as they talked about the outside. What use was that? It was all very well being sentimental, but survival required pragmatism. Besides, getting too close to the above-grounder might make their own position shakier. They couldn't jeopardise getting a permanent place.

Thirdwun Nebam yelled, 'The pots are about to boil over.'

Some of the toolwuns sniggered.

'By the Pit!' Delvina jumped up, rushed over to the hob and lifted the lid. She stirred the pot and then ladled boiled snails, cave shrimps and shredded tree roots into copper bowls.

Retza's mouth watered at the tangy smell and his stomach rumbled. The above-grounder was right, algae cakes hardly stuck to the ribs. If they were lucky, there'd be some left for them too. With a shrug, he went back to his scrubbing.

Delvina flashed him a smile as she walked past balancing a tray weighed down with the brimming bowls. She rapped against the door of the ward room.

Retza scrubbed harder, ignoring the growling of his stomach. The best food went to the Lead Hand and her henchwuns and then to the toolwuns. Being a probationary prentice was not a whole lot different from being a drudge. They landed all the grubby and unwanted tasks and the worst rations. At least he and Delvina were learning the job and, if they passed their probation, they had a chance of becoming toolwuns one day. Then things would be different.

He was sloshing the black, scungy scrubbing water into the outlet pipe when someone hammered on the outside door.

From where he was sitting in recreation area, the Thirdwun put his hand over the dice cup. 'Don't just stand there, get the door, slug.'

Retza bit down a retort. Dipping his head, he opened the door to another messenger in the Overseer's livery. The Lead Hand appeared from the ward room and took the cylinder from the young messenger. A furrow deepened between her pale eyebrows as her eyes flitted across the message etched into the foil. Her face tightened. Surely she wasn't frightened? Retza gripped the bucket handle, the thin metal cutting into his calloused palms.

Looking up, the Lead Hand scanned the room. 'Thirdwun Nebam, you're in charge.' She beckoned the other two henchwuns and marched out of the crib, Secondwun Putarn and the Scrybe close behind her. The Thirdwun turned back to the game with his cronies.

Retza dropped the bucket and, ignoring Delvina's startled look, slipped out after the Lead Hand. He had to find out what was happening. The door thudded behind him, a whisper of air on the back of his neck. He swallowed hard. He wasn't really doing anything wrong. It was the end of his shift after all. Why shouldn't he take a stroll along the Causeway? Though it was strange to be without Delvina.

Keeping to the wall and the shadows as much as possible, he darted after them. Lead Hands of the other Crews jostled past him, heading in the same direction. The above-grounder was right. If the Overseer had called another emergency meeting, something serious was happening. The leadwuns of the Greenstone South Crew reached the end of the Great Causeway and ascended ladders to upper echelons and the Overseer's Domain. Dashing out from a recessed doorway, Retza put his foot on the lowest step.

A hand gripped his shoulder. 'What are you up to, drudge? Crewless don't belong here.'

A burly watcher in black glared at him from beneath the rim of his hood.

Retza stuck out his chin. 'I'm a trywun of the Greenstone South Crew.'

'Woopy-do.' The man twirled his baton then, with a blur, whacked Retza's upper arm and back. 'Get back to your crib, little tryhard, before I need to teach you a painful lesson.'

Swallowing against the sudden tightness in his throat, Retza stumbled backwards. As soon as the watcher's back was turned he ducked into an alcove. Rubbing his throbbing shoulder, he loitered in the shadows, keeping out of sight of the watchers.

Hours later, the gong sounded for the start of the third shift. The Lead Hand and her henchwuns hadn't reappeared, but he had to get back for his duty. With a last glance over his shoulder, he sprinted back to the Greenstone South's crib.

As he ducked into the door, Nebam cuffed his ear. 'You're late. Hurry up and grab your kit, grub.'

Delvina grimaced and fell in beside him. Rather than heading for the cages to the mining shafts deep below, Nebam led them into the upper layers to shovel bio-mass sludge into the glimmer trucks. It was hard work and dirty. When they finally got back to the crib, Retza showered with the others and fell into his bunk. His limbs were like dead weights and his eyelids heavy, but he couldn't sleep.

In the years since his parents had died, he'd assumed that if only he and Delvina could get a berth in a crew, they'd be safe. Now nothing seemed certain. He squirmed on the firm bunk. The glimmer lights couldn't fail. The Overseer said the Dark Ones would protect them.

The next day, in the off shift time, Nebam had them scrounging the storerooms for old cloth and pieces of frayed rope which they plaited, twisted and dipped into the oily sludge. Retza's gut twisted. If the glimmer lights failed, they would need the primitive torches. Surely the Glimmer Heart could not fail. The Dark Ones would protect them.

And still the Lead Head had not returned from the Overseer's Domain.

Zadeki started out of a light sleep and pulled his mantle about him. A horn was blasting in the distance. The strange blue lights were dimmer than usual as the Darane snored in their bunks. It was hard to keep track of time in these benighted tunnels but it must be close to ten days since he had left his kin-group to fly over the mountain. An act of bold defiance he now regretted. Instead of proving to the Kinleader and his parents that he was capable enough to be a pathfinder, he had gotten himself stuck in an impossible situation where even they wouldn't be able to find him.

Every time the Crew left for their shifts, a couple remained behind to guard him. And despite all his questions and careful listening, he had found no other way out of this grim underground realm than the Cauldron. At least Delvina was friendly. Maker help him, the weight of the mountain and the lack of wind and light was suffocating. How he longed for a breath of fresh air on his face, the smell of green things and the sky stretching high above him.

He tried to scratch his arm where it itched beneath the split. The Scrybe Barekia had suggested it would take forty days for the bones to heal, but his people healed much faster than that. The ends were already knitting together. Better to keep that to himself though. Soon he would be able to shapeshift again—and then he'd escape, find the way to the Cauldron and fly home.

Leaning against the cool stone wall, he felt the vibration against his backbone. He put his ear against the wall. Almost below perception, a shuffling sound came from the distance. Then the sound of urgent boots striking the Causeway. Moments after, the door clicked and swung open, revealing the Lead Hand and her henchwuns.

She nodded to Putarn. 'Get them up and be quick about it.' She dashed into her quarters, while Putarn banged the gong and shouted. 'Wake up, get your kits.'

The Darane tumbled out of their bunks, eyes blinking owlishly, muttering and swearing.

Retza's colourless eyes narrowed in speculation. 'What's going on, Secondwun?'

The older Darane clouted the youngster. 'Do as you're told, slug.'

Barekia turned around from where she was pulling an old glimmer torch, make-shift torches and medical supplies out of the recessed lockers. 'The Overseer has ordered a full muster. We need to be at the Grand Cavern by the start of next shift.'

Groans and more curses filled the room, but underlying the protests was the timbre of fear. The lights flickered once again, and a shudder ran through the crib. One of the littlewuns, visiting from the crèche, began to whimper.

A tremor ran through Zadeki. Perhaps next time the lights wouldn't come back on. He took a deep breath. If he could control his dislike of the deep darkness under the mountain, maybe he could use the confusion to escape. He glanced at the twins, their faces pale and strained and shook his head. It wasn't as though he could help the

Darane in their self-imposed predicament anyway. It had been ten days, a half cycle of the silver moon, Argenti. He needed to get home to the forests and find his kin.

Putarn loomed over Zadeki and pulled him to his feet with rough hands. The sour smell of sweat, unwashed clothes and rock dust assaulted his senses.

'Maybe it's time you earned all the food we've wasted on you.'

Barekia frowned. 'He is still healing.'

'Maybe he can't use his arm, but he can still carry a pannier on his back. You, girl,' he pointed to Delvina. 'Load up rations and water for us all to last a day or two and don't spare the freeloader. Scrybe, have you got the torches and tinder box? Good!'

'Sorry,' Delvina whispered to Zadeki, standing on tiptoes as she tried to strap the pannier on him. 'Do you mind kneeling?' she muttered after a minute or two.

He grunted. So he was a pack animal now? He rolled his shoulders, loosening his joints. The harness was not too tight. Perhaps he could still shapeshift. If not, he'd have to wait until they got to their destination—wherever that was in this dark realm. Hopefully it would be closer to the surface.

'Keep still.' Delvina's tone was not unkind.

She packed the provisions into the conical basket pressing into his back. Hurried movements filled the room. The pannier was almost full when the lights flickered and went out. A startled gasp, then silence as movement ceased. An orange red flame flared into life. Garish shadows danced on Barekia's wrinkled face as she held up one of the makeshift torches.

Putarn hastily lit another. He growled. 'Keep moving, you lumps of coal.'

The next few moments were chaotic as toolwuns grabbed their packs.

Havilah appeared, a bag over her shoulder. 'Let's move out.'

Nebam shoved a couple of slower toolwuns in line. 'Keep together.'

Zadeki followed close behind Retza and Delvina as they shuffled out the door. The Greenstone South crew joined the Darane streaming along the Causeway towards the north, the whites of their eyes reflecting the glimmer of hundreds of flaming torches and the eerie blue of the occasional glimmer torch. Zadeki felt like a giant towering over them. He lowered his head and hunched over as much as the heavy basket allowed, hoping to be less conspicuous. Maybe he would help the twins and even old Barekia if he could, but whatever happened, it was time to get out of this dying realm.

Delvina sank thankfully down onto the smooth stone floor. Her muscles were weary after the forced march through the flickering dark. The huge cavern was packed with the People; lead hands, henchwuns, toolwuns of the other shifts, crèches, even drudges with their rickety young and a few old ones. Each crew had its own allotted place and hooded watchers, truncheons in hand, stood in the shadows around the edges. She wrinkled her nose at the sour stench of frightened bodies crammed together and an acrid grey smoke drifting from the torches and small fires scattered around the large space. When they had entered the cavern, the high roof had been threaded with the tiny lights of the glow worms. Now the expanse above them was black as soot, whether from the noise or the smoke, Delvina wasn't sure.

Retza hunched down, his arms brushing hers, and squeezed her shoulder. 'The Overseer will know what to do.'

'Opening the great doors to the outside would be a good start.' Zadeki sat cross-legged on the floor half a pace away, his head resting on the wall and the pannier leaning drunkenly beside him.

Delvina shivered. The strange light of the moons and the white world of the Cauldron had haunted her dreams. If the moons could dazzle them, what would the sun do? 'The outside is dangerous for us.'

Retza stiffened. 'Shush. That's forbidden talk.' He pointed to Barekia walking towards them, handing out dry algae cakes and sips of water.

The moments dragged on as the air grew staler, even in this huge cavern. Delvina slumped against her twin, her head resting on his warm shoulder. Before they'd joined the crew, they had huddled together in the commons like this many a night, with empty bellies, half-alert for the patrolling watchers and rival crewless wanting to steal their spot.

Hours later a gong sounded, jerking Delvina out of a fitful sleep. She pushed herself up into a sitting position, rubbing her eyes and stretching her back. Surely it was sometime in the first shift of a new day. Others were beginning to stir from sleep as the watchers moved among the clustered groups, calling them to attention.

With a whumff, a circle of bright blue light flooded the balcony high up on the west wall. A hush fell over the crowd. First, black clad watchers with whips and batons appeared, positioning themselves at the four corners of the balcony. Then Overseer Uzza stepped out.

A thousand flashes of coloured light sparkled from

the gems encrusting his flowing garments and his elaborately plaited hair and beard. Behind him stood his henchwuns, mate and seven offspring, five grown and two littlewuns.

One of the Overseer's henchwuns, Speaker Elim, stepped forward and thumped an intricately carved metal staff on the floor of the balcony. 'Listen to the words of our great leader, favoured of the Dark Ones.'

Delvina curled her fingers tighter around Retza's hand, then found and gripped Zadeki's hand on the other side of her.

Overseer Uzza cleared his throat. 'People of the Glittering Realms, over the last couple of centuries the Dark Ones have protected us against our enemies. They have provided us …'

Zadeki's long fingers curled in hers. 'What enemies?'

'Hush,' Retza hissed.

'… shelter, water, food.' The Overseer's voice boomed on, trailing echoes whispering after his words.

Zadeki brought his mouth close to her ears. 'Who are these Dark Ones?'

She frowned at him. 'The dwellers of the shadows, the makers of the caverns and the People.'

The above-grounder looked sceptical. 'You are children of the Maker—he sang the stars, our world and all its inhabitants into being. He looks after us.'

Retza snorted. 'Doesn't appear he's been looking after you.'

This time Putarn cuffed her brother's ear. 'Quiet. You disrespect the Overseer.'

'… and they have given us light.'

A sigh ran like flame through the gathered People.

'But now, the Dark Ones are angry with us. They have

taken the light from us and they demand a price. For they are hungry.'

Tendrils of cold crept through Delvina's gut. A great murmuring vibrated about the cavern.

The Speaker banged the staff. 'Silence. Let the Grand Overseer speak.'

'Each crew must choose two youngwuns—a male and a female—to be given to the Dark Ones. This is a sad duty, but necessary for our survival and an honour to the ones chosen. Choose and prepare them well. Any crew that withholds their youngwuns will face the full anger of the Dark Ones.'

With that the Overseer turned and disappeared back into the gaping door behind him. His entourage followed.

Putarn's arm fell on Delvina's shoulder, while the other draped over Retza's. 'I guess we can thank the Dark Ones you two decided to join us.'

Zadeki stood up tall, his eyes like dark pools in his luminous face. 'I'll go.'

Zadeki clamped his mouth shut. Why had he said that? Whatever fate the Darane Overseer planned for the 'chosen', it couldn't be pleasant. But it was a chance to get the pannier off his back, to get away from this crowd. *And maybe you can help these people.* He shook his head. But what could he do? He couldn't even fly over a mountain without getting himself into trouble.

Putarn thrust his face forward, his breath hot and rancid on Zadeki's cheeks. 'Even better. Why sacrifice a strong hand when we have a useless freeloader to spare?'

'But, he's not from our People.' Delvina swallowed. Then she looked at Retza, her eyes anguished. 'But I guess ...' she dropped her gaze to her sturdy boots, pressing the back of her hand against her mouth.

Havilah stood behind the Secondwun, her face strained, her mouth a grim line. Nebam and Barekia moved up beside her. Retza grabbed Havilah's sleeves. 'You can't do this. You can't take my sister.' He dropped to his knees. 'Please. I'll go.'

The Lead Hand's purple eyes glistened, whether with fear or pity, Zadeki wasn't sure. She covered her neck with a trembling hand.

Putarn's brow furrowed, his mauve eyes narrowed. 'Matu ...' he cleared his throat. 'Leadwun, you heard the Overseer. We have to select a boy and a girl—youngwuns. Who else is there? It has to be her, everyone else is too old.'

Nebam stroked his scrappy ginger beard, his narrow face crinkled into a thoughtful frown. 'Terrible it may be, but isn't it better that these two quench the Dark Ones' wrath, than the whole Crew be lost to the Overseer's retribution?' He almost looked apologetic.

Scrybe Barekia muttered under her breath. 'Or feed young Uzza's madness, rather.'

The Lead Hand's nostrils flared. 'Hush, oldwun. Don't let the watchers hear you speak such forbidden talk.' Putting her hands in her sleeves, she seemed to shrivel. 'I'm sorry, Retza, my sons are right, we have no choice, two must go.' She turned to Zadeki. 'Are you sure you wish to take Retza's place?'

A tremor ran through Zadeki. The Darane milled all around him, the air full of their whispering and subdued weeping. If he shapesifted, he'd be overcome by sheer numbers before he got far. He had to get away from the crowds. And the time of waiting was over.

He pulled in a lungful of fusty air. 'Can't you do something to stop it? If all or even most of the crews ...'

'They wouldn't, for fear of the Dark Ones. And if they did, the watchers surround us. If I knew of another way ...'

Barekia folded her arms, her jaw set. 'The Glimmer Heart ...'

Havilah turned, her hands palm upwards. 'Even if the Crystal Heart could be fixed, there is no way we could reach it. The watchers would stop us before we even got to the first door.'

This was his only way out. If Havilah had been prepared to resist he would help, but what did he know of crystal hearts or glimmer lights? He would do what he could to save Delvina and, if he could do nothing, at least Retza would live. Zadeki bowed his head 'I'm willing to go, earth mother.'

'You honour us. Perhaps the powers above sent you.'

Zadeki's heart stilled. Could it be by the Maker's will that he was here? He thrust away the thought. It was his own stupidity that got him into this predicament.

Havilah brushed Delvina's shoulder with the back of a work-worn hand. 'Barekia speaks truth. This is not the way of our ancestors. I would take your place if I were still a maiden, but I have no choice. I must think of the whole crew.'

Straightening her shoulders, Delvina took Zadeki's hand in her own, her fingers cold and trembling like baby birds ... 'I too am ready to serve.'

'Then Putarn and Nebam, take them to the alcove and prepare them for the ceremony. And make sure you treat them with the respect they deserve.'

Emptiness filled Retza.

It was as if his thoughts were blanketed with that strange white stuff—snow Zadeki called it. How could he live without his twin? Even when everyone else had abandoned them, they had had each other.

Nebam and some other toolwuns were preparing Delvina and Zadeki behind a skimpy felt screen—scrubbing them with precious soap and scented oils, plaiting their hair with gems and dressing them in fine tunics of white cotton as though they were leadwuns. Someone had removed the splint from Zadeki's arm. Putarn stood nearby, with a smirk on his face. All around the cavern, the other crews were preparing the youngwuns they'd selected. He shouldn't have allowed the above-grounder to take his place. Whatever happened, he and Delvina should be together. Maybe it wasn't too late.

He edged towards where the Lead Hand stood, arms folded, listening to Scrybe Barekia.

The old woman spoke in a fierce whisper. 'Havilah you should listen to me. The Overseer would be better letting a techwun examine the Glimmer Crystal Heart than this nonsense.'

The Lead Hand sliced her hand down in a dismissive motion. 'He won't hear of it. You know that.'

Retza blurted out. 'Besides, there are no techwuns left.' The two women turned. He shuffled his feet as they pinned him with stern eyes.

At last, Barekia nodded. 'Aye, the Dark Ones demanded the techwuns' blood when I was a prentice. My father was one of the first to die. If I could reach the Crystal Heart that powers the glimmer lights, maybe I could do something.' She crossed her arms across her shrunken chest, her wrinkled face settling into grim lines.

'Havilah, you were such a plucky youngwun. Remember your resolve. You've become too afraid. Too ready to let those boys of yours have their way.'

The Lead Hand's amethyst eyes flared. 'And the last time ...'

'Havilah, you were not to blame, Uzza and that fool Gilarth were. The deaths of Ozier and ... the others ... were not your fault. But my son wouldn't want more youngwuns be fed to that tyrant's delusions. What happens when the sacrifice doesn't bring back the glimmer lights? More blood, more sacrifices.' She heaved a breath. 'Besides, no point sifting through the slagheaps of the past when there a fresh mineral vein to be dug. We have to try at least and not give into more of this madness.'

Indecision flitted across the Lead Hand's face. Her shoulders sagged. 'What can one crew do against so many?' She pointed to the hooded figures against the wall. 'He has hundreds of watchers bonded to him and ready to do his will. And you know my sons won't help.'

'Better to die trying to save our people. This charade only prolongs the end.'

Was it possible to fix the Crystal Heart? Then surely the Overseer would have done that. And would it be enough to save Delvina? He had to find a way or ... he swallowed hard ... or die with her.

Putarn and Nebam approached, flanking the two chosen. Tears brimmed on Delvina's white lashes. Zadeki's silver face was set like stone.

Retza wrung his hands. 'At least let me go with my sister instead of the above-grounder.'

'It's too late for that. Now hush both of you.'

'We're ready to present the sacrifices, Lead Hand.' The Secondwun's eyes flicked at Delvina and Zadeki before sliding away to study the floor.

Putarn thrust out his beard, the pale ochre strands catching the torch light. 'Unless you would like to challenge the Overseer's authority, Leadwun, we must hurry. We are already the last to contribute.'

The Lead Hand's gaze swept over Delvina and Zadeki and nodded. She turned to her sons and squared her shoulders. 'Thank you. The Scrybe and I will take them to the place of offering.'

The Secondwun frowned, a look of unease crossing his surly face. 'The watchers won't like it.'

'Maybe, but if I must order this thing, then I'll carry it out myself.'

Her hand brushed against Retza's arm. 'Come with us.'

The black mouth of the tunnel directly under the Overseer's Balcony gaped in front of them. Zadeki tilted his head against the unfamiliar weight of adornments in his hair. The conviction grew stronger with each step—that the way out of the underground realm lay ahead of him and that he needed to help these doomed youngsters. Two watchers flanked the entrance, their pale grey eyes gleaming in the shadow of their black hoods.

One stepped out to bar their way. 'We will take it from here. Your presence isn't required, Leadwun.'

The Lead Hand pulled Retza forward. 'He's the girl's family.'

'This is irregular.' The watcher twirled the truncheon.

Barekia mumbled, 'By ancient right, family have precedence when their loved ones are on the brink of sorrow's dark river. Should the chosen be treated with less respect than a common worker?'

The guard hesitated, glanced at his companion. 'What harm can it do?'

When the other man shrugged, he stepped aside. 'Very well, but make it quick.'

A long dark shaft reached out into the heart of the mountain. A breath of air caressed Zadeki's face and his heart quickened. Somewhere among the maze of passageways there were openings to the outside world. Delvina's hands trembled in his, her breath sharp beside him. Retza's hot breath tickled the back of his arms. Zadeki stumbled on a ridge in the floor and he gripped Delvina's shoulder to steady himself.

Havilah touched his elbow. 'Careful.' She turned to Barekia. 'Where is the Glimmer Heart from here?' She pitched her voice low.

The old Scrybe's voice came in a gruff whisper behind him. 'The passageway divides two hundred paces ahead. The cage goes up to the Overseer's Domain, to the left is the Sunken Temple of the Dark Ones and the path to the right leads to the Crystal Glimmer Heart.'

'Can you fix it, Barekia?'

'I can't be sure until I see what the problem is. Maybe.'

They walked in silence along the tunnel until up ahead, where it joined with another at right angles, the vague outlines of hooded watchers blended in the shadows. Zadeki's heart rate accelerated. It might be too soon after his injury, but he had to shapeshift.

'Two of them, four of us,' he said. 'They are only lightly armed.'

Retza let out a breath. 'We have no weapons, not even our pickaxes or shovels.'

Havilah stopped walking. 'Then our hands and our

muscles will have to do. Retza and I ...'

There wasn't time for discussion. Zadeki loped forward. He knew this transformation better than the eagle one. Stretching out, he felt the bones, muscles and skin change. The mended bone in his arm held. He bounded along the corridor, his great padded feet making a bare whisper of noise on the stone, his jaguar's eyes drinking up the light, seeing the Darane with ease. He pounced on the watcher on the right knocking him senseless with a swipe of his paw, barely feeling the strike of his companion's truncheon. He twisted around and wrapped his forelegs around the second man's neck, pulling him down. By then, the others had caught up with him. They pulled the watchers away, using the men's own cloaks and belts to gag and bind them.

Barekia approached him, her hands shaking. 'You said you could not shapeshift with broken bones.'

He grinned. Her eyes rounded and she took a hasty step backwards. The other three were looking at him, faces as grey as ash.

'It's a risk, but my bones are mending.'

Havilah gave a tremulous smile. 'To think you were sleeping on the floor of our crib each night. It's a wonder we weren't devoured in our bunks. Can we trust you?'

He sat back on his haunches. He could leave them to their internal struggles. He had done his best for the twins. His throat rumbled with a low growl. The Overseer was a madman. How many young people would die pointless deaths today? And, with the gates closed off and their power gone, perhaps they would all perish. Not that it was his responsibility. *But maybe you are here for a reason.*

He tilted his large feline head and twitched his tail. 'If

your plan is to rescue these youngsters, then I'll help.'

The Lead Hand wrinkled her forehead. 'I hadn't planned to. There would be too many watchers in the temple, and it is vital to get the Heart working again. It's not just the lights, but our ventilation, water supplies and glimmer trucks as well. Without these we cannot survive as a people.'

'You could leave the tunnels.'

Delvina stepped forward, brushing his fur with her stumpy fingers. 'We can save both the Heart and the chosen youngwuns. How far is the Crystal Room?'

Barekia took a deep breath. 'Not far. See me safely there, Adelphi, and you should still have time to save the chosen.' She turned to Havilah. 'A rescue attempt would provide a distraction.'

The Lead Hand nodded sharply. 'Then let's not waste time. Retza find an alcove to hide these two watchers and then catch up. Barekia, show Zadeki the way.'

Delvina's eyes widened in wonder at the Crystal Heart at the centre of the Glimmer Room. The room was large, though not as large as the Grand Cavern. It contained contraptions of metal discs, cogs and an arrangement of giant crystals as well as pipes, wires and other things she could not name. She wrapped her arms around her chest in a tight hug. So this was the beating heart that kept the Glittering Realms alive?

There had been no watchers outside the door and they had used the captured truncheons and a liftbar Retza had found in an alcove to break down the locked door. The old Scrybe hadn't wasted any time in examining the mysterious machine. The Lead Hand and

Retza hovered over her shoulder, watching as she tapped a crystal here or pulled out a cog or cylinder there. A huge black jaguar with coal black eyes prowled near the door.

'Can you see the problem?' Havilah drummed a truncheon against her legs.

'Give me time.' Barekia's eyes focused on the crystal machine. 'Once there were three hearts. The other two failed decades ago.'

The great black cat coughed. 'I'm glad you understand it, earth mother, but it's time for me to go.'

The tip of his tail twitched and his coal black eyes gleamed in the shadows. Delvina looked away from the jaguar's murderous looking teeth and swallowed hard. This was Zadeki, her friend. He was on their side.

Havilah stopped her drumming. 'I'll come with you. The twins can guard Barekia.' She pulled on a hooded watcher's cloak and helmet, taken from one of the guards. 'The longer we distract them the better.'

Cold clutched Delvina's stomach at the Lead Hand's grim face and determined tone. There would be at least as many watchers as chosen, guarding them as they were sacrificed and thrown into the pit to feed the Dark Ones. Two against so many ... Delvina stepped forward. 'I'll come too.'

Retza spun round. 'No! Delvina, you can't. You are safe here.'

She could see the fear in his eyes. He had always protected her, ever since they had been on their own. But how could she allow Zadeki to risk his life, if she wasn't willing to do the same? She walked up to her brother and wrapped her arms around him. 'I have to do this.'

He stood rigid in her embrace. 'Then I'm coming too.'

Havilah shook her head. 'Someone must stay to guard

the Scrybe. Best it be you, Trywun Retza.'

Zadeki bounded over and rubbed his head up against them, almost knocking both of them over. 'As chosen sacrifices, we'll attract less suspicion.' His voice was deep, resonant, yet still it sounded like the above-grounder they'd brought from the Cauldron.

Retza's face scrunched up, lips pulled back from his teeth. He shoved the big head away. 'You're a cat. You don't look like a sacrifice.'

Zadeki's tail lashed. With a spring, he reared up, his powerful arms and great paws extended. Retza stumbled backwards, pulling Delvina with him as Zadeki's shape shivered and wavered, flowing into the form of a tall silvery-skinned adolescent, jewelled headdress and garment barely out of place.

Delvina gasped, the hairs on the back of her neck standing erect. 'How do you do that?'

'With all this extra weight?' The stones tinkled as he tilted his head. 'With difficulty, but I think I've just enough energy for another transformation. Come, we're wasting time.'

Delvina released her twin. 'I'll be alright, Retza. I have to do this.'

'Let's go.' The Lead Hand threw a truncheon to Delvina, who caught it neatly and tucked it in her gold belt at the back.

This was it. She glanced at Retza, blinking away tears, a liftbar in his hand, and Barekia, the tip of her tongue peeking out of her parted lips as she tapped on another gleaming crystal. Turning her face toward the twisted door, Delvina stepped through into the corridor shrouded in shadows.

Zadeki pushed back the exhaustion, his muscles vibrating with tension. He'd never done two transformations without replenishing his energy stores. He'd never had to fight before this day either. How many watchers would there be? What if he failed as he had in the snow storm? Delvina walked beside him, her presence warm and solid. Behind them, Havilah's breathing came in unsteady hitches. Each step brought them closer to danger.

A muted babble of voices mixed with soft moans came from the end of the long corridor. The two watchers standing at the door stepped forward to bar their way.

The watcher on the right smacked his truncheon into his palm, the whack echoing down the dank corridor. 'You're late Greenstone South. Any longer and the Overseer would have sent you and your crew to the lower cesspits as drudges.'

Havilah dipped her head. 'The girl's brother was distressed at his sister's fate and took considerable persuasion to let her go.'

The other guard, with a squashed nose, hawked and spat on the tunnel floor. 'He should be glad he's not sharing it.'

The guards tipped back their heads and crowed with laughter. Taking advantage of their distraction, Zadeki edged closer and wrenched the whip from the second guard's belt. Gripping it two-handed, he wrapped it around the man's throat, cutting his braying off with a jerk. The man's eyes bulged, fingers scrabbling at the plaited leather thong at his neck.

The first guard charged at Zadeki, smashing into him. Delvina pulled out the truncheon from under her tunic and stuck him from behind until he crumpled to the ground.

The second guard's frantic movement slowed. Zadeki eased up on the whip and felt for a pulse. The man would live. He helped Havilah tie and gag the men.

Leaning against the stone wall, Delvina pressed the back of her hand against her mouth. He knew how she felt. Swallowing the sourness at the back of his throat, he turned his face away from the guards trussed up against the wall, one inert, the other moving weakly. His people were not warriors. They did not kill, not unless innocent lives were at risk. There would be more watchers beyond the door and young lives to defend.

He gripped Delvina's shoulder. 'Ready?'

She ran a calloused hand over her broad face. 'Yes.' Her voice was a hoarse whisper.

Havilah nodded. 'You two go first. I'll stay in the shadows.'

Together, they pulled open the door and entered. The room was painted with torch light and shadows, smoke curling lazily upwards to the open roof and the cavern ceiling high above them. Watchers stood around the painted stone walls and the chosen in front of them, with bare feet and plain tunics as white as bleached bone, their hair plaited and adorned with jewels.

Havilah, in the shadows behind, put her lips to his ear. 'There, the pit.' She pointed towards the end of the long rectangular room. In front of an obsidian altar, a large gilded grating was set in the polished stone floor, taking up the centre of the room.

Zadeki tipped his head back. The ceiling had been removed so that the room was open to the bigger cavern above it. Toolwuns, drudges, even the youngsters crowded around the edge, peering down with eyes wide and lips parted. Silent and grim. In one area Putarn and

Nebam stood with the rest of the Greenstone South Crew. At other end, on a small platform on the far side above the temple, the Overseer filled a large metal chair, its twisted, carved surface reflecting the red flame of the smoking torches. The Darane leader tapped his ring encrusted fingers on the carved armrest.

'The last of the chosen, your Eminence,' Havilah called out, deepening her voice to sound like one of the Watchers at the door.

The Overseer straightened in the chair, his ash grey eyes narrowing to slits.

'Greenstone South. Your tardiness is noted.' A scrybe sitting on a small stool beside him hastily scratched away in an open book as the Overseer continued, 'Start the ceremony.'

A small gong chimed. Two veiled women, swathed in dark cloth, entered from a door at the other end of the sunken room. Chanting and swaying, they carried bowls of incense, sweet soporific smoke drifting and curling around them. A man with a blue-dyed beard and tattooed face stepped out between them, his midnight blue robes flowing over his corpulent form. He launched into a long speech about the Dark Ones, their mercy and grace and the need to appease their anger.

The priest droned on, meticulously going through the elaborate ritual with the help of the silent women. Zadeki edged closer to them, shoving down his growing anger. What kind of 'gods' were these that demanded the blood of the young to appease them? How could these people believe such filth? His muscles were coiled and aching to stretch into action, but they had agreed, only when the chosen's lives were in danger would they attack, so as to give Barekia more time to repair the Crystal Glimmer

Heart. Only then could the Overseer's power be challenged and the young Daranes' lives be saved.

Retza stalked the perimeters of the dim room, his body as tense as weighted chain. He should be with his twin, with Delvina. What if Zadeki and the Lead Hand failed to protect her? Despite his reservations, it had been the right thing to rescue the above-grounder. He was powerful, dangerous even, but willing to help them. Yet, even in the big cat form, how many watchers could he defeat before their numbers overwhelmed him, even with the help of the two women? *So why would your presence make a difference?* He balled his fists and growled at his inner voice.

'Can you stop pacing? You're distracting me.' Barekia looked up, a strand of white hair escaped her messy plait. 'Here, make yourself useful. Get me the wrench.'

Grumbling, he grabbed it from the tool recess and brought it to her. 'Can you fix it?'

She reached up a hand without taking her eyes off the mechanism. 'I'm not really a techwun. I watched my baba as he worked but that was a long time ago.' She loosened some bolts and removed another panel. 'It's a mess in here. Uzza hasn't let anyone with knowledge near the thing in decades. He's as bat-crazy as his father was.'

Retza's skin prickled at the trash talk. If the watchers heard ... He grimaced. Idiot, he'd already crossed the line. 'If you can't fix the Heart then ...'

She reached into the cavity, feeling small levers and cogs. 'Everything looks in order. Maybe the problem is further up.' The fine wrinkles on her lined face deepened.

Retza chewed his lip. Whatever the technical

problems, he couldn't help her. 'I'm wasting my time here. I'm going to help the Lead Hand.'

Barkeia rocked back on her heels. 'Relax, young trywun. Your sister is in good ... paws.' She chuckled, then when he didn't smile, shrugged. 'That young Adelphi is powerful as a dozen watchers.'

He shook his head, impatient at the platitudes. 'There are more than ...' He stopped, tilting his head.

A rapid pounding boomed along the passageway outside the door, getting louder by the moment. He gripped the cold iron of the liftbar, his hand shaking. Boots. Someone running towards them. More than one.

Barekia yelled. 'Shut the door.'

Pushing against the inertia, he sprinted towards the entrance and shoved against the twisted remains of the iron door. It was half off its hinges, and the corner screeched as it dug into the stone. At halfway it stuck. Even as he heaved against it, two guards tried to cram through the narrow gap barely wide enough for one of them.

'I told you the scum were up to something,' the snaggle-toothed one snarled.

The taller one behind lashed his whip, the end snaking past his companion's head and wrapping around Retza's wrist. Fire seared through him. He yelped, fumbling the liftbar before taking a tighter hold.

Ignoring the pain and resisting the pull of the whip, he transferred the liftbar to his other hand and slammed the end into the first watcher's face. The man's nose crunched and blood spurted in a crimson spray. Retza brought his knee up into the man's groin, instincts sharpened from past patch fights in the commons. The man fell groaning to the floor, wedged between the door and the jamb.

Retza grabbed the plaited leather of the whip and pulled the other watcher towards him. The man dug his heels in and swung down his truncheon at Retza's head. Retza ducked back behind the door, the heavy rod glancing off his raised elbow. He howled with pain.

'Do you need help?' Barekia called.

'No, just fix the Heart.' Retza's grip on the liftbar was slick with sweat and his heart raced. What if the watchers had found Barekia unprotected?

Sucking in air, he dodged another swing from the truncheon. Before the man could recover his balance, Retza struck hard, metal connecting with the man's thick skull with a sickening thump. The watcher crumpled to the ground on top of the first. Dropping the bar, Retza stood with hands on knees, panting and sweat rolling down his face.

The sound of boots striking stone once again echoed from the direction of the Grand Cavern. Not more guards!

Barekia's hoarse shout echoed through the room. 'I think I've found the problem. There's a blockage in the intake tubes, a small avalanche maybe connected to the snow storm you youngwuns saw. Can you help?'

A quick glance showed her perched on a ladder balanced on the large pipes disappearing into the roof. Retza wiped the sweat and splattered blood off his face. 'Expecting more company,' he rasped.

He kicked the moaning guards back into the tunnel, put his back to the jammed outer door and heaved, but it wouldn't budge. Maybe he could use the liftbar as a lever. He snatched it up. Even as he angled it, dark figures loomed out of the shadows just paces away from the door. He grit his teeth and raised the liftbar. 'Come any closer and I'll crush your brains.'

'Peace, slug. We've come to help you.'

Nebam and some other toolwuns from the Greenstone South crew stepped into the flickering torchlight.

Was it true? Retza's legs went weak. He leant against the door, shudders running through his body.

Nebam gripped his shoulder, his mauve eyes widening at the gleaming crystals of the Heart and the two battered guards slumped against the wall in the passageway. 'Looks like you didn't need it. You've done the Greenstone Crew proud, Prentice Retza.'

Retza's chest swelled at the title. Not a trywun anymore, an acknowledged prentice. Then the image of Delvina's pale face flashed before him. Ice clutched his heart. 'Have they started the sacrifices yet?'

'No, not when we left,' one of the toolwuns, Danel, said.

Nebam stroked his sparse beard. 'Priest Beltain was nearing the end of his spiel. Soon, I'd say, lad.'

Barekia's strident voice cut across the room. 'If you've finished congratulating yourselves, get yourselves over here. I need your help if I'm to get the Heart started.'

As Nebam and the others jostled past him, Retza collapsed to the ground. Soon as he could breathe, he had to get to the temple.

Delvina shivered, reliving the dull crunching sound of her truncheon bashing into the watcher's head, the metallic smell of blood. She hid her shaking hands in her tunic. She'd never raised her hand against another before. Had she killed him? Even if she hadn't, he might not survive his injuries. She swallowed hard. Retza always teased her for rescuing cave animals instead of adding them to the food bag. She didn't want to hurt anyone, but she couldn't let the Overseer steal the lives of the frightened young prentices and other youngwuns crowded around the walls of the Sunken Temple. If she did nothing, wasn't she also guilty of their pointless deaths?

Driving her nails into her palms, she forced the memories of the man's bloodied scalp and sickly groan from her mind, and focused on the droning voice at the other end of the room. Zadeki, moving with the stealth of quicksilver, had worked his way level with the grating. One of the torches had begun to smoulder, the acrid smoke stinging her eyes. Finally, the priest's foul words fluttered into silence.

A gong filled the space until her teeth vibrated with the sound. With a ponderous dignity, the priest lifted a golden bowl from the altar for the people to see before handing it to a watcher.

He then drew an obsidian knife from his waist sash. 'Remove the grate.'

Two of the watchers rushed to push the metal covering aside, revealing a pit filled with black night. A sulphurous stench emanated from the gaping hole. Taking a white stone from the altar, the priest dropped it into the dark maw and waited until a faint splash echoed below, many heartbeats later.

The well-fed priest lifted his soft hands, the long dark knife reflecting the flickering flames of the torches. Chills ran down her back. She had been just a littlewun when the last sacrifices had been made to appease the anger of the Dark Ones after the cave-in that had taken the lives of her parents. But only a few youngwuns had been taken that time. Now two from each crib lined the walls, twenty-eight in all. More than twice that number of watchers lurked behind them.

Priest Beltain intoned in a sing-song voice, 'Awake, oh Dark Ones, awake and feast. To you we give these chosen ones.'

The priestesses swayed, swinging the incense and chanting in unison. 'Give us your benison.'

Heads bowed, hands over their eyes, the spectators above echoed the words. A rising heat burned Delvina's neck and cheeks. How could they just comply? These were their sons and daughters that the Overseer had condemned to the knife and the pit.

The servant of the Dark Ones beckoned to a girl with two long straw-toned plaits who stood nearest to him. Shudders ran through her shapely body. A watcher caught her by the elbow, pressing her down until she knelt at the altar. Another exposed her pale throat.

Delvina shot a look at Zadeki. Surely, there was no more time. He gave a curt nod and leaped, his long, slender body stretching out into feline form. The white gowned youngsters scrambled out of his way, huddling back against the walls as he loped past them and bowled over Priest Beltain. The black glassy knife spun into the air, clattering against the wall. The priestesses dropped the bowls, spilling the aromatic oils and ash. Watchers elbowed their way through the chosen towards the great cat, cracking their whips or twirling their truncheons. Others stood uncertain against the wall.

'Stop, stop this sacrilege at once.' Overseer Uzza lurched to his feet, his voice booming out above them.

Havilah pulled down her hood, exposing her face. A gasp ran through the crowd. Delvina stood in front of her, gripping two truncheons, ready to defend her leadwun from the watchers.

Havilah stretched up her arms and called out, her voice carrying clearly. 'Uzza son of Hezikah, this is a travesty. Killing our children will not bring back the light but only steep darkness in our hearts.'

The Overseer's face darkened. 'Lies, all lies. People of the Glittering Realms, only by appeasing the Dark Ones can we restore the light. Don't you see, these crazed and wicked women are in league with an evil shapeshifter and threaten us all? We will be condemned to the dark forever.'

A groan ran through the crowd. From where he stood with the Greenstone Crew on the rim, Putarn's voice rang out, 'Matu, listen to our wise leader. Don't anger the Dark Ones.'

The Lead Hand raised her arms and shouted. 'I am not the crazed one. Even now my scrybe works as a techwun to restore the Heart that powers the glimmer lights.'

The Overseer grabbed the staff from Speaker Elim and thumped it on the dais. 'She will doom us all with her deceptions. Throw her in the pit with her foul companions or the darkness will take us. Chosen Ones—what is the point of saving your own lives, only to die with your families in the long dark?'

Some of the chosen began to mutter to each other. A voice cried out, 'Kill the traitors.'

A number of the watchers backed away from where they were crowding around Zadeki and headed towards Delvina and the Lead Hand, shouldering the milling youngwuns out of the way. The closest one lunged to grab Havilah. Without thinking, Delvina swung her truncheon across his face and dodged the blows of another.

One by one, people above joined in the chant. 'Kill them, kill them.'

Zadeki could smell the dank terror of the foul priest squirming beneath his great paws. He could snap the man's neck or crush his skull in an instant. Surely the black-hearted follower of the Dark Ones deserved to die, yet even this charlatan was a child of a Maker. He peeled back his lips in a deep-throated growl that rumbled from his throat to his chest. The man groaned and fainted. Zadeki spun around, swerving and dodging the blows as watchers pressed in on him. He charged at the ones in front. Some slipped in their rush to avoid him and fell screaming into the pit.

He had to reach the women. Ignoring the blows from the others, Zadeki pushed towards where Delvina stood back to back with Havilah, fending off attacks from the watchers and some of the chosen.

Havilah stood panting, a strand of honeyed hair across her face and a bruise purpling on her cheekbone. She shook her truncheon. 'It is time the harsh rule of the Dark Ones ended. Decide for yourselves, who is right—if you would have freedom, then today is the day to fight for it. Stand with us.'

Shaking off a couple of watchers grasping his fur, Zadeki called out in his deep jaguar voice. 'Uzza speaks nonsense. How can the Dark Ones give you Light? Only the Maker of Light can do that.'

A muttering swept through the people above them. The girl with the long plaits scrambled to her feet, a young man helping her. 'They are right. What sort of gods are these?' She and several of the chosen ran up and shoved the watchers, distracting them and allowing Zadeki to reach Havilah and Delvina.

Most of the younglings scrambled out of the way, some even joining the attack.

The constant battering of truncheons, fists and boots was beginning to take its toll on Zadeki. Though he hated the thought, perhaps it was time to unsheathe teeth and claws, to do more than nip and push. Another watcher piled on top of him, pulling him to the ground.

The sounds of boots came from the passageway. The door swung open and Retza rushed in, followed by Nebam and another toolwun, Danel. Together, they thrusted aside watchers and chosen.

'She's fixed it!' Retza yelled.

Then, a humming sound vibrated through the stone under his paws. A blinding, flickering flash of blue lightning. The glimmer lights flared back into life, illuminating the sunken shrine and the Grand Cavern above with a cold blue light. Around the pit, watchers and chosen froze like statues. Slowly, wonder seeped onto their faces.

Zadeki roared. Pushing up, he shook off his attackers.

Uzza gripped his staff, 'See, see the Dark Ones have blessed us despite your rebellion.'

Havilah laughed. 'No, my Scrybe has fixed the Heart.'

Thirdwun Nebam shouted. 'Lead Hand Havilah is right. No sacrifices were made but the lights have come on. The Overseer is a liar and a fraud.'

A murmur ran through the crowd. The Overseer quailed as the many turned and advanced towards him, muttering and hissing.

'Imbeciles, you will regret this. Those that are loyal will be rewarded. Those that disobey will be cursed.' With that he backed away, most of his council and the watchers bunching around him, keeping the angry crowd back with their truncheons and whips.

The watchers left standing in the Sunken Temple dropped their weapons and put their hands behind their heads in surrender.

Delvina whooped and rushed at Zadeki, throwing her arms around his neck. 'She did it. We did it.'

'We did.' He grinned pulling Delvina, Retza and Havilah into a huge feline hug.

Retza blinked at the pinkish-gold glow at the end of the tunnel. A chill breeze caressed his cheeks and lifted his hair. This time the smell was more aromatic and woody. Apprehension crawled in his stomach. Taking a deep breath, he stepped out into the Cauldron, Delvina and Zadeki following close behind.

He shielded his eyes against the brightness. Remnants of snow draped over the dark green branches of tall, conical trees and filled the hollows between grey boulders and the steep walls of the Cauldron. Each little detail from the lumpy texture of the tree bark to the knobs and crevices of the rock was picked out in exquisite detail. Above the sheer cliff walls and angular snow-covered peaks, rays of light radiated from a point on the eastern horizon, painting the expanse in swirling layers of gold, orange, and crimson edged with purple.

Delvina clutched his jerkin, her rapid breaths loud in his ear. 'Is this what day looks like?'

Zadeki let out a bubble of laughter. 'Not quite. The sun is just below the horizon. And look,' he pointed to the darker west. 'Argenti, the silver moon, is setting. More than fifteen days have passed since I collided with this mountain.'

Retza rubbed the fuzz on his chin. So much had happened in that time. Overseer Uzza had escaped in the tunnels, but all remaining leadwuns had insisted that Havilah should be the Acting Overseer. Havilah's first act was to give Barekia the title of Techwun, urging her to take charge of the Crystal Glimmer Heart and to train prentice techwuns. Now Zadeki was leaving for his kin. It felt like losing a limb.

'You could stay, above-grounder. You could help hunt Uzza out.' Retza cleared his throat. 'We couldn't have defeated him without you.'

Zadeki clapped him on the shoulder. 'You don't need my help now, earth-biter—or should I say, Prentice Retza?' His teeth flashed in a grin. Stooping down, he threw his long arms around Delvina, holding her tight for a second. 'Well, time to go, I guess.'

Delvina sniffed, her face burnished by the strange light. 'I know you need to go home to your family but you will come back for a visit?'

'Yes, I think I will.' Releasing his grip on Delvina, Zadeki stepped back. He gripped Retza's arm. 'And you, both of you, are welcome to visit my kin.'

Retza swallowed against the lump in his throat. 'Maybe we will. When we work out how to open the front gates.' Though the outside still seemed a place of danger.

His twin snorted. 'Barekia says that could take decades with so many blocks, locks and traps set upon it but we could start using the Cauldron again—to grow food and to get used to the outside.'

A silence fell between them. Retza had so much he wanted to say, but couldn't find the words. He fiddled with his belt. A flash of brown feathers, a small bird alighted on the drooping branch of one of the trees. It tipped its head back and opened its beak, letting out a long melodious trill.

Zadeki stepped back, a wild joy in his dark eyes. 'My home is calling me. The Maker be with you.' Then with a nod, he ran along the icy ground towards the eastern rock face, leapt into the air and stretched out his arms. His outline shimmered and flowed until a great eagle with fierce mien, white crest and dark grey wings launched into the wind currents. With powerful downstrokes, he spiralled higher and higher before flying towards the sunrise.

Delvina grabbed Retza's hand and leaned against him, his warmth a comfort in this strange place. As the eagle dwindled to a dark speck, a searing golden light peeped over the horizon.

The End.

Acknowledgements

I originally wrote Heart of the Mountain for the *Glimpses of Light* anthology, but it soon took on a life of its own and grew too big for the designated word limit. I loved the story and have developed it into a short novella.

It is the first in the adventurous tales of young Zadeki. The events of this story occur many years after 'Ruhanna's Flight' (my eventual successful submission for *Glimpses of Light)* but a few centuries before the events of the *Akrad's Legacy* series and the other Tamrin Tales (such as 'Fever', 'The Herbalist's Daughter' and 'Lakwi's Lament').

The story, in part, is inspired by other great story tellers such as J R R Tolkien, Jeanne DuPrau's *City of Ember*, Frances Hardinge's *A Face Like Glass*, Christopher Paolini's *Eragon* and my own vivid memories of descending into the depths in an Underground tour of Mt Isa Mines, Mt Isa. I have endeavoured to make this story my own.

My heartfelt thanks to my wonderful editors, Nola Passmore (of *The Write Flourish*), Paula Vince and to my redoubtable critique partners and beta readers Nicole Nugent, Kathleen Hillenberg, Suzanne Hay-Bartlem, Raelene Purtill, Julian Green.

I also had fun with the cover design and appreciate the tough and truthful critiques of my young artists in residence, as well as suggestions from Suzanne Hay-Bartlem, Kathleen Hillenberg, Christina Aitken, the Swinburne Creative Writing Critical Friends and the Omega Writers Science-Fiction and Fantasy Groups.

I'm especially grateful for my family—my loving husband Tony, my precious children, my parents Tom and Jean Curtis—who instilled in me a love of faith and fantasy—and siblings, Tom Curtis, Frank Curtis, Chris Curtis and Kathleen Hillenberg, whom I've shared many wonderful adventures.

Most of all, I'm grateful to my Maker in whose creative footsteps I can only hope to follow.

Jeanette O'Hagan July 2016

About the Author

Jeanette O'Hagan enjoys writing fiction, poetry, blogging and editing. She is writing her *Akrad's Legacy* Series—a Young Adult secondary world fantasy fiction with adventure, courtly intrigue and romantic elements. Her short stories and poems are published in a number of anthologies including *Glimpses of Light, Another Time Another Place* and *Like a Girl*.

Jeanette has practised medicine, studied communication, history, theology and, more recently, a Master's in writing. She is a member of a number of writers groups. She loves reading, painting, travel, catching up for coffee with friends and pondering the meaning of life. Jeanette lives in Brisbane with her husband and children.

Check out the social media of your choice—though Jeanette is most active on *Facebook, Twitter, GoodReads* and *Instagram. Amazon Central* has all her books in one.

Or you can browse her webpage—Jeanette O'Hagan Writes http://jeanetteohagan.com or sign up to the email newsletter for the latest news on releases and events - http://eepurl.com/bbLJKT.

Author Note

Enjoyed *Heart of the Mountain*? Why not leave a fair and honest review on Amazon, Goodreads and/or your favourite reviewing site. Writing reviews (no matter how short), helps support authors to keep on creating and publishing the stories you enjoy.

The story of the twins and Zadeki continues in the sequel, *Blood Crystal*. Now avialble on Amazon and other outlets.

Coming Soon

Stone of the Sea: a novella (*Under the Mountain* series)
Akrad's Children—the first in the Akrad's Legacy series

Blood Crystal: a novella

The underground realm is under attack from ousted Overseer Uzza. The Crystal Heart is failing and twins Delvina and Retza must brave a dangerous journey to find the key to survival.

Will they reach the Zadeki and his people in time. Will they find anyone alive when they return? Unless the twins and Zadeki act, the realm under the mountain will fall. Can they save it in time and at what cost ?

Blood Crystal is the second novella in the Under the Mountain series. Set in the world of Nardva.

Amazon: https://www.amazon.com/dp/B073H83F42/
Elsewhere: https://www.books2read.com/u/3yPBwV

www.ingramcontent.com/pod-product-compliance
Lightning Source LLC
Chambersburg PA
CBHW020623120726
47905CB00003B/917